You can read this way up!

OWL BAT BAT OWL

Marie-Louise Fitzpatrick

WALKER BOOKS
AND SUBSIDIARIES

LONDON · BOSTON · SYDNEY · AUCKLAND

Or ... you can read this way up!

For Michael, because it all began with him. xxx

First published 2016 by Walker Books Ltd, 87 Vauxhall Walk, London SE11 5HJ • © 2016 Marie-Louise Fitzpatrick • 10 9 8 7 6 5 4 3 2 1
British Library Cataloguing in Publication Data: a catalogue record for this book is available from the British Library • ISBN 978-1-4063-6439-2 • www.walker.co.uk

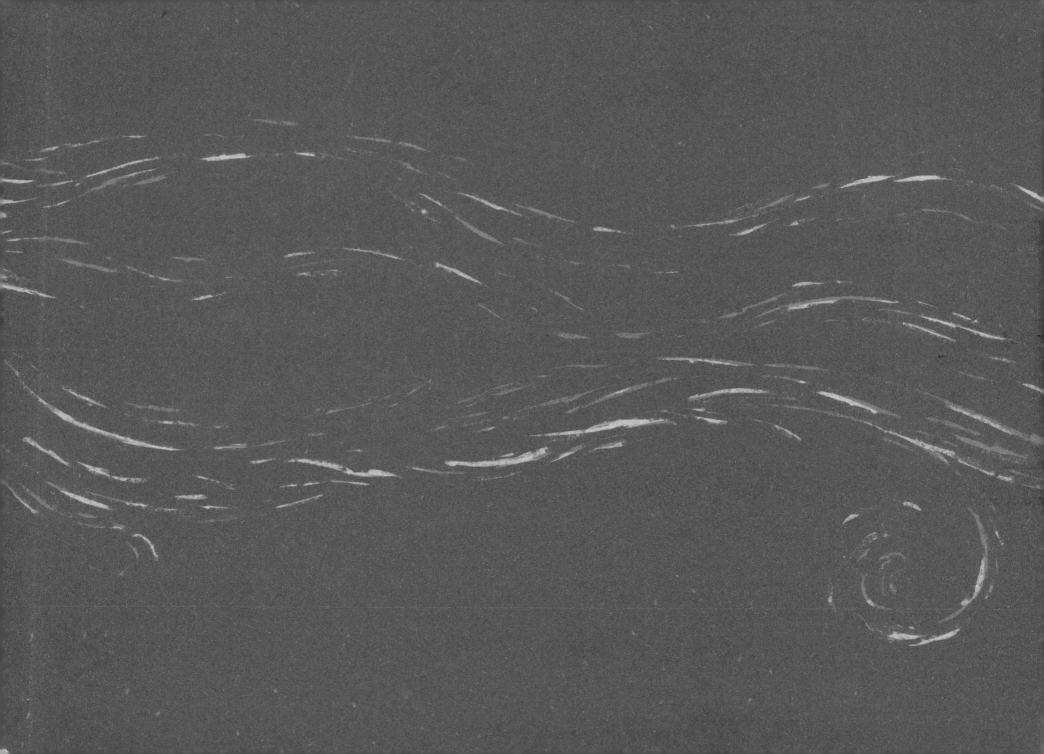